The How To Become a Fairy Handbook

Editor: Brooke Vitale
Illustrator: Katrina Santucci
Designer: Lee-May Lim

Text and Illustration copyright © Shane Barbanel 2021

For information, contact: Mom n Dad Designs LLC
1024 Broadway, Woodmere NY 11598

ISBN 978-1-7368061-0-4

The How To Become a Fairy Handbook

By Gili Guggenheim

Once upon a time there was a princess,

Princess Emunah.

Princess Emunah lived with her Mum and Dad – the king and queen – and her little sister, Princess Rosy.

Princess Emunah liked being a princess, but what she really, truly, ever so wanted was to be was a fairy.

"Because fairies are blue and pink, fairies sparkle and fly, and they are pretty."

The princess dreamed of fairies, she sketched and painted fairies in her sketchbook.

She talked about
fairies a lot!

So she asked,

and asked,

and asked,

and asked her Mum if she could meet the Queen of the Fairies and find out if she could become a fairy someday.

The Queen knew that girls from all over the kingdom wanted to become fairies, and only the very best would be considered.

Being a princess did not give Emunah a better chance than anyone else. But still, she did seem to want it quite badly so after a great deal of thought, the Queen finally said, "I will talk to the Queen of the Fairies, but first you will need to show me that you deserve such a big gift."

Princess Emunah jumped up into the air!

"Thank you!
Thank you!
Thank you Mum!!!
she cried.

"Yes!!
Yes,
yes, yes,
yes, yes,

I will do **anything** you ask!"

"What do you want me
to do Mummy?"

"**Very well**" her mother said.

"You will need to clean your room, make your bed, put away your toys, be nice to your sister, and do what your Father and I ask you do - the first time - for seven days and nights. Then I will talk to the Queen of the Fairies for you."

Princess Emunah
thought hard.

She counted the days.

She imagined the work.

Finally, she said

"Seven days is a really looooong time Mum!"

At that, the queen started for the door. "If you don't want to meet the Queen of the Fairies..."

"Okay!
Okay, okay, okay.
Okay!"

Princess Emunah shouted.

"Okay, I will clean my room, make my bed, put away my toys, and do what you and Dad say. "

"And be nice to your sister,"

the queen added.

"Of course Mummy!
And be nice to Rosy."

At first the going
was slow.

Princess Emunah
hated cleaning
her room, but
she did it.

She put away her
toys and made her
bed, and even let
Rosy do her hair.

And though she
grumbled and groaned,
she finished her chores
again and again.

Then something magical happened. Princess Emunah realized she felt proud of herself.

She was happy that her room was clean, and that she was the one who cleaned it!

She looked at her made bed and felt good knowing she was the one who made it.

And being hugged by her sister Rosie
turned out pretty great!

On the seventh night,
as Princess Emunah slept,
a warm glow filled her room.

The glow grew brighter
and brighter until at last
it woke the princess.

Princess Emunah opened her eyes to find a fairy floating in the middle of her room!

"Are you...?" Princess Emunah started.

The fairy nodded. "Yes, yes... I am the Queen of the Fairies. I've seen how hard you've been working this last week and I've come to have a chat with you."

"Are you here to give me wings?"
Princess Emunah asked.

"Are you going to teach me to fly,
and be a fairy?"

The Fairy Queen smiled.
"How do you think fairies fly?"

Princess Emunah thought hard about it.

"With their wings?" she said finally.
"Well, yes and no," the queen said.

"Our wings help us move through the air,
but what really allows us to fly
is our quality."

"Quality?"

Princess Emunah asked confused.

"Yes, you see fairies fly because of the actions
we take. It's because of what we do in the
world, and how we are on the inside that counts.
The more good we do the lighter we become until
we can soar! It's our good qualities that give us
our power, not what we look like."

"Wow! I never knew that,"
Princess Emunah said.

"But what kind of good qualities?"

"Well, kindness is one," the queen said.

"Kindness?"

said Princess Emunah with great attention.

"Yes, kindness is not just being friendly
once because your mom asked you to.
It's being kind even when you don't want
to be. That can be hard sometimes.
But being kind to those closest to you and
even those not-so-close, makes us lighter."

"I can do that,"
Princess Emunah said.

"What else?"

"Another quality is generosity,"
the Queen of the Fairies said.

"Generosity

is kindness with giving attached. For example, when you see that your sister is sad because you are eating a cookie and she has none. Generosity is sharing some of your cookie with her. It's kindness in action."

"I've done that before!"
Princess Emunah cried.

"Indeed you have," the queen said.

"...and your generosity did not go unnoticed. In fact as I recall it was your generosity that made your sister stop crying."

"Of course those things alone are not enough. Another very important quality fairies have that helps us fly, is respect," the queen said.

"Respect?" said the princess.

The queen nodded.
"Respect means treating others as you would like to be treated. Some people, like your aunts, uncles, and others such as grand wizards & witches earn our respect for what they've learned, achieved and accomplished. We honor them with our attention and we give them our ears and eyes so that we may learn from them."

"That sounds hard,"
Princess Emunah said.

"It can be," said the queen.
"But listening to what they say and watching what they do helps us to grow and to be more like them."

Understanding the fairy queen,
Princess Emunah replied,
"I guess I never thought of it that way."

"Letting our talent show makes us lighter too," the queen continued.

"What's a talent?" Princess Emunah asked.

"Our talents are those things that make our hearts sing, such as dancing, painting, building with blocks, fitting together puzzles, climbing, or creating stories. The things that make our hearts sing are different for everyone, but if you do find it and nurture it, you will grow lighter and lighter."

"Forgiveness

is important too," the queen said.

"Sometimes people do things that upset us, or hurt us, but they don't do it on purpose. Forgiving them means not making them feel bad for their mistake and not reminding them of what they did."

"Like when Rosey got paint all over my drawings?" Princess Emunah asked.

Smiling the queen said, "Exactly. You forgave her. You knew she didn't do it on purpose and she felt bad."

"You know all those things my Mum made me do – clean my room, make my bed, be nice to my sister. They were hard to do at first, but the more I did them the easier they got," Princess Emunah said.

"That's right," said the fairy queen "and as you do these things – do as your parents ask, treat others with kindness, let your talent shine – you will find that you start to float."

"So I can fly?"
the princess asked.

"Yes, you can indeed, Princess Emunah."
the queen replied.

"When you act as fairies do, you will find yourself getting lighter and lighter, you will begin to float, on that day I will appear to you again to help you grow and learn further."

As the princess watched,
the queen of the fairies
shimmered and flew off.

The princess climbed back into her bed and pulled the covers up to her chin. As she drifted off to sleep, a smile crossed her face as she knew she was on her way to becoming a fairy.

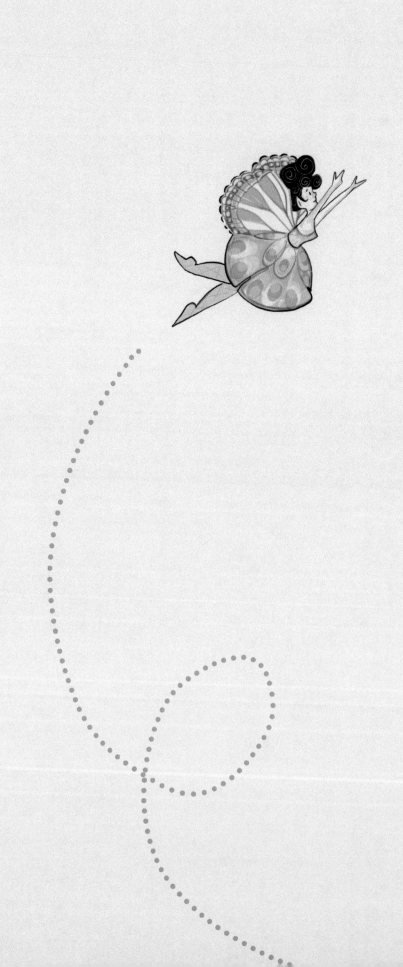

Made in the USA
Middletown, DE
02 September 2021